Levi &
Liam,
Stay Silly! :)
Joe Barton

For Emma

You are my heart. ♥

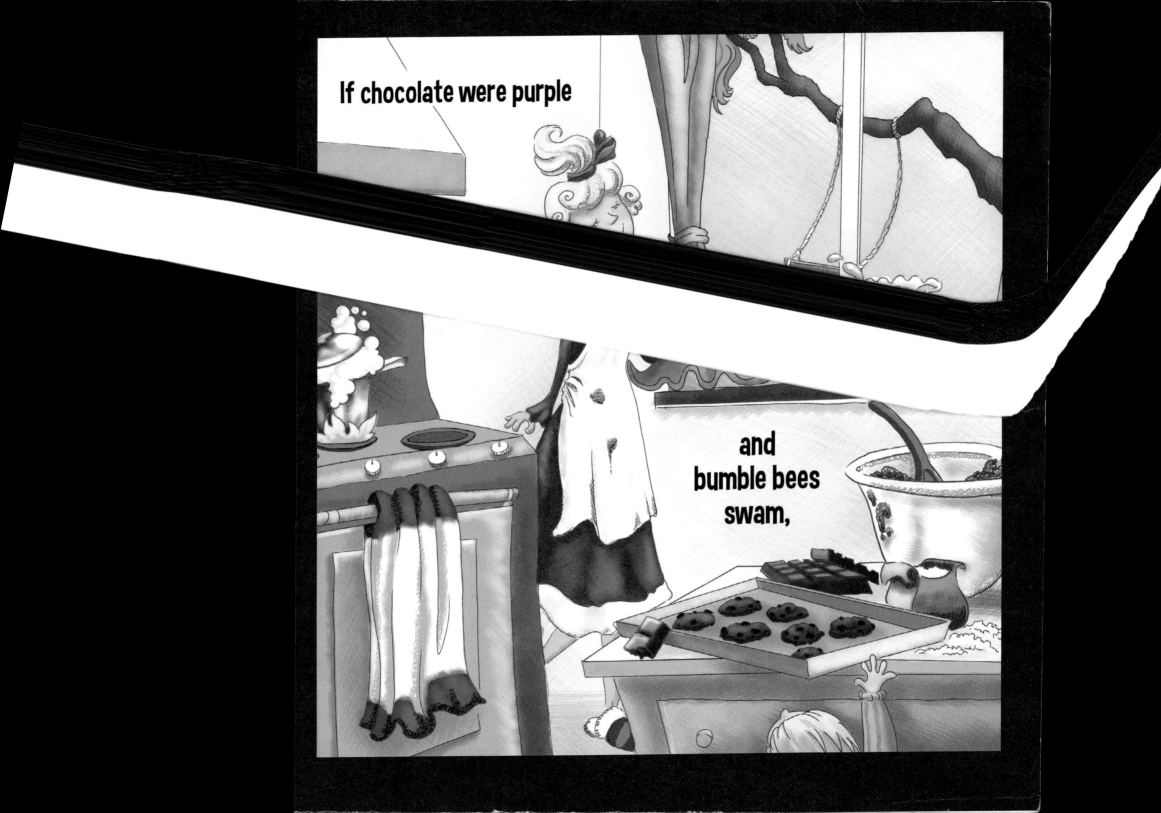

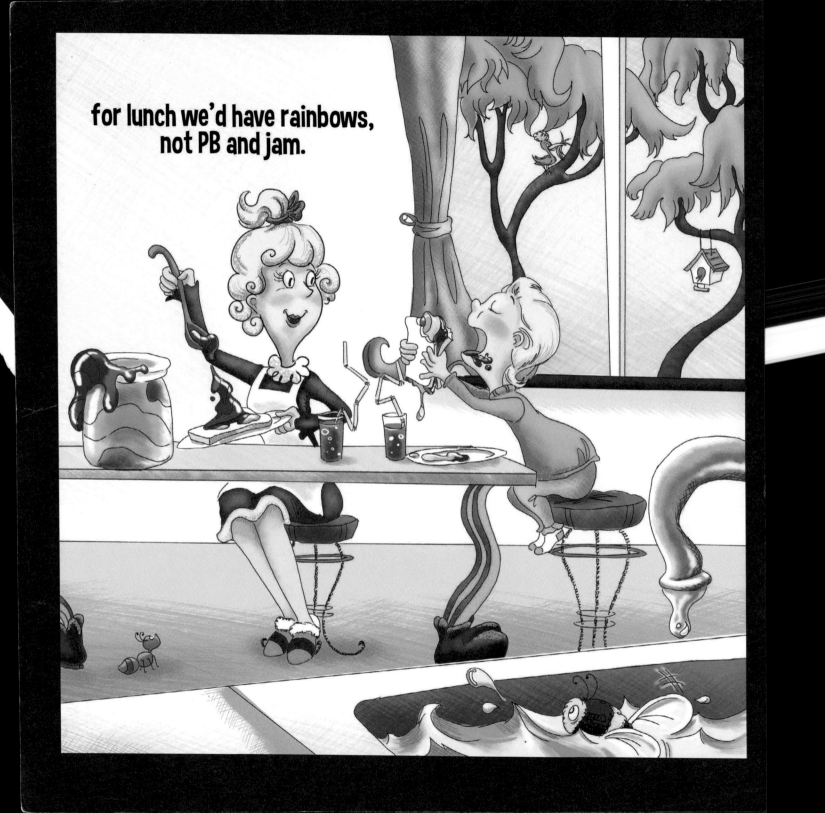

We'd bounce to the beach
on legs made of springs,

and visit a lizard
who dances and sings.

If dolphins could fly
and seashells could wink,

our time at the shore
might look silly, I think.

Some fish would have hair—
golden and curly,

If bananas were round
and glowed in the dark,

we'd eat them at night,
walking home through the park.

And after our dinner
of rocketship stew

I'd wrap you in jammies
from Kalamazoo.

If the story we read
about Whiskery Willows

made you flop
down and
wiggle your pillows,

so teddy bear dreams
could soon fill your head.

If the sky whispered softly
as the stars hummed a tune,

they'd sing you to sleep
by the light of the moon.

And if you were scared
by thoughts in your head

two lollipop soldiers
would stand by your bed.

and everything changes
from all that we know

I'd still hold you close
and watch over you

31308806R00018

Made in the USA
San Bernardino, CA
06 March 2016